$4.50

This book belongs to Firefighter

Fireman Sam™ Annual 1994 is published by **The Redan Company Ltd.**, 29 St John's Lane, London EC1M 4BJ. **Fireman Sam,** including all prominent characters featured in this annual, and the distinctive likenessess thereof, are trademarks and copyright © of **Prism Art and Design Ltd**, 1986 and 1993.
All rights reserved.
Printed in Belgium by **PROOST**

Contents

The New Power Hose!

Two exciting parcels arrived at the Fire Station one morning. "What's in them?" asked Elvis.

"It's our new high powered water hose," explained Station Officer Steele, proudly.

The high powered hose was a little too strong. It squirted water all over Steele. **Splossh!**

Sam tried the new power hose too, but it just sprayed water all over him. **Splossh!**

A Listen and Look Story

The hose spun round and around. It was out of control. Elvis tried to run away but it soaked him too.

"Don't worry men," said Steele to the soaking fire-fighters. "In the second box, you'll find our new uniforms."

After the firemen had got out of their wet things, Fireman Sam proudly opened the second box...

...but it was full of...**dresses!** The postman had delivered the wrong box to the fire station!

7

Oh dear! Poor Norman is ...

Lost in the Fog!

Fireman Sam woke up one morning and looked out of his window. To his surprise, he couldn't see **anything!**

"Great fires of London!" he gasped. "A thick fog has fallen during the night. I can hardly see in front of my nose!"

Sam wrapped up warmly and set off to work. It wasn't easy making his way up to the Pontypandy Fire Station. The fog was so dense that he could hardly see where he was going. "At least there won't be any emergencies today," thought Sam.

"Who would be silly enough to go out in weather like this?"

Meanwhile, Naughty Norman Price was setting off on an expedition! "I'm going to explore the lost world of Pontypandy," he decided, sneaking out of the General Store into the gloomy fog. "This fog makes it look as if we're on another planet!" Silly Norman was soon lost in the fog. He had wandered out of the village, into the hill-side but now he couldn't see in which direction the village lay. "**Ooh** this is **spooky!**" he wailed, peering into the grey fog. "I want to go home!"

Dilys soon noticed that

Norman had going missing and had 'phoned the fire brigade. Fireman Sam was busy checking Jupiter's compartment when the alarm sounded. "**Lost boy in Pontypandy!**" cried Station Officer Steele, over the loud speaker.

weather like this! The fog is thicker than ever!"

"Where are we, Sam?" asked Elvis, half an hour later. They had travelled up and down the roads outside Pontypandy, trying to find Norman. All they had discovered was a deep, muddy hole that Sam stepped into. "I don't know," groaned Sam, peering through the murky fog. "I've got a horrible feeling that **we're** lost now!"

"All firefighters to start searching immediately."

"Great fires of London!" gasped Sam, as the firefighters left the fire station in pairs. "Fancy Norman going out in

Penny Morris and Trevor were in trouble too! They had taken a wrong turning and had ended up in a bramble bush!

"Ouch!" cried Trevor, pulling himself free. "Well, Norman's not in there, that's for sure!"

"And it's not the way to Pontypandy, either!" sighed Penny. "I haven't a clue where we are!"

Steele was getting worried. His firefighters had been gone a long time. He decided to search for them himself! In his pocket he carried a small whistle. Each time he reached the end of a road, he blew the whistle, very hard.

"Hello? Is anyone there?" called a small frightened voice. It was Norman Price. He was very glad to be found!

Steele continued to blow his whistle. Sam and Elvis heard it and came running up. So did Penny and Trevor.

"**Whew!** I'm glad to be rescued!" said Sam. "But I wonder where we are?"

"You're in Pontypandy!" said Dilys, coming up to them. "You must have been walking in circles! I could hear that whistle blowing for ages!"

Dilys invited them all to stay until the fog lifted. "And as a special treat, I'll make some delicious **pea soup**!" she said.

Sam laughed. "Well that sounds like more fun than the **pea-souper** outside!" he chuckled.

PHEEP!

FACE PAINTING!

Materials

Make sure:
Check that face paints are non-toxic and that you are not allergic to it.

You will need:
Face paint crayons (these can be found in most toy shops) or borrow old make-up.

A moisturiser, like baby lotion. Rub it on your face before painting and it will wash off easier.

Norman's Tiger

Use a sponge to colour your face all over with yellow paint.

With a black crayon, draw a black nose and whiskers.

Finally, draw lots of tiger stripes in black or brown.

James' Skeleton

Use a sponge to colour your face all over with white face paint.

Draw big black rings around your eyes, and a small triangle on your nose.

With a black pencil, draw a wide, toothy smile.

Sarah's Clown

Use a sponge to colour your face white.

With a black pencil, draw a small triangle over each eye.

Draw a big, red nose, or use your plastic nose from Red Nose Day.

Lastly, draw a big smile around your face.

The Fishing Trip!

Trevor was taking Naughty Norman Price fishing. They set off for the river in Trevor's bus.

By the river side Trevor suddenly swerved to avoid a duck walking across the road.

Splosh! The bus fell right into the river. "What shall we do?" asked Norman who was feeling a little frightened.

Trevor and Norman climbed onto the roof of the bus and then swam to the side of the river.

A Naughty Norman Story

Trevor found a telephone and dialled 999. Sam answered the call. "Don't worry, Trevor, I'm on my way."

Sam and Steele soon arrived in Jupiter and quickly tied a towing rope from the back of Jupiter to the bus.

Starting Jupiter's engine, Sam soon pulled Trevor's bus out of the water. "It will just need to dry out."

In the back of the bus, they found a fish! "We caught a fish, after all!" laughed Norman.

The Bicycle!

The Firefighters of Pontypandy head to the rescue on a ...bike!

Spring had arrived in Pontypandy. Fireman Sam was walking home through the park, watching the twins riding their bicycles.

"I used to love riding a bike when I was young," he thought. "And I know Trevor and Penny had bikes too. Wouldn't it be fun if we had a bike that we could **all** ride on!"

This gave Sam one of his inspired ideas. He hurried home and spent the evening working in his Inventing Shed. Next morning he arrived at work on a very strange looking bike. "It's a four seater tandem," he explained to Firefighter Penny Morris, who stared in surprise at the long bike. It had **four** seats!

"Now we can all go for a ride together, after work," Sam said, parking his bike in the yard. "It will be a great laugh - and good exercise for us, too!"

Station Officer Steele had bad news. "Jupiter's starting motor is cracked. We'll have to order a new one. Until then, she will have to remain in the shed."

"I hope that we won't need Jupiter before she's fixed," said Sam. "We'll be stuck if someone calls the fire brigade for help!"

In Pontypandy, Bella Lasagne was doing just that!

"**Mama Mia!**" she cried, struggling to pull herself out of an empty lard barrel. "I'm-a stuck!"

Bella had been working in the cellar, standing on a stepladder to clean the shelves. The ladder wasn't very steady and Bella had toppled backwards, landing bottom-first in the wooden barrel. Now she couldn't pull herself free!

Luckily, she was carrying a portable telephone in the pocket of her overalls. She dialled 999 and asked for the fire service!

At Pontypandy Fire Station, Officer Steele didn't know what to do!

"How can we rescue Mrs Lasagne when we don't have a fire engine to

get us there?" he groaned.
Sam smiled. "We can use
my bike," he suggested.
"With four of us pedalling, it
won't take us long to get
to the village."

With Sam in front, and
Penny, Trevor and Elvis
riding behind him, the four
firefighters set off on Sam's
strange bike. They
pedalled very fast, down
the hill
towards
Pontypandy.
"I think that
we're going a
bit too fast,
Sam," gasped
Penny.

Sam pulled on the
brakes ... but nothing
happened!

"**Great Fires of
London**!" cried Sam, as the
bike went even faster. "We
can't **stop**!"

Suddenly, the bike split
in two, with Sam and
Penny going one way, and
Trevor and Elvis crashing
into a hedge!

"**Waah!**"
cried Penny,
as the two
tandems
wobbled
across the
road!
"**Yikes!**"

18

gasped Sam, when the front wheel detached itself from the bike and raced the tandem towards the village!

Sam struggled to keep the bike upright as they swept into the village ... but it was no use! The bike hit a bump and Sam and Penny went flying into the air!

They landed beside each other in boxes of squashy tomatoes outside the General Store!

"What is going on?" demanded Dilys, coming out. "I can't sell those tomatoes **now**. They were squashed and now they're flattened!"

Sam explained that the firefighters had come to rescue Bella.

"Bellisimo! There's no need!" said Bella, coming out of the store. "Mrs Price, she-a heard me shouting and rescued me herself!" "Oh **no**," groaned Penny, struggling to pull herself free of the box. "All that effort for nothing!"

Sam sighed. "Well, it's taught me to keep away from bikes! From now on, I will travel **only** in Jupiter!"

vase of flowers

chair

mouse

cat

jacket

helmet

Look carefully at the picture on the other side and then **colour** in the things that you see.

It's Fun to Count ...

Colours

How many **red** things can you find in the picture? Put your answer in the red box. Now count the **blue**, **green** and **yellow** things.

There are [ ] **red things**

There are [ ] **blue things**

There are [ ] **yellow things**

There are [ ] **green things**

22

The Decorating Machine!

Sam invents a marvellous machine to take all the hard work out of decorating!

Firefighter Penny Morris had asked Sam to decorate her living room. "Leave it to me," said Sam who had a soft spot for Penny.

Sam went straight home to his Inventing Shed. "Decorating the old way is too slow," he thought, as he tinkered about with lots of mechanical odds and ends. "I shall invent a machine that will do all the work in a couple of

minutes." Sam worked very hard - he even forgot to eat his dinner - and soon his invention was completed.

"This is my Decorating Machine," he told an amazed Penny, when he arrived on her doorstep, that afternoon. The machine looked very odd, with mechanical arms, spray attachments and buckets of paste and paint brushes fixed to its sides. Penny had never seen anything quite like it.

"I'll have all the decorating finished by the time you return home from work," Sam told Penny who was on Watch Duty at the Pontypandy Fire Station. "I think you'll be surprised when you next see your living room!"

When Penny had gone, Sam set to work. He pressed a button on his invention and stood well back. The Decorating

Machine rumbled into life. First, it tore off the old wall paper before pulling out a sheet of new wallpaper from its compartment. It then pasted it with a paint brush and carefully stuck it against the wall.

But Sam noticed that some of the paste had splashed onto his invention and dribbled inside the machinery. This glued up the circuit boards, and sent the Decorating Machine **crazy!**

"**Hey!** Hold **on!**" spluttered Sam, as the machine slapped paste all down his face and jumper. "You're supposed to paste the **walls** - not **me!**"

Sam's invention took hold of him in its mechanical hands and pushed him against the wall. As Sam struggled to break free, the machine pasted a sheet of wallpaper down his back!

"**Help!**" shouted Sam, pulling his way out of the wallpaper. He tried to reach for the off button but the machine pulled out three tins of paint and a paint brush, and painted Sam in rainbow colours instead!

"**Great Fires of London!**" spluttered Sam, backing off as the machine whizzed around the room, painting and pasting everything in sight. "It's out of control. I'd better 'phone for the fire service!"

Penny received Sam's urgent call at the fire station. It wasn't long before she was parking Jupiter outside her house.

"I'll need this net, this axe and this fire extinguisher," Sam said, taking the tools from Jupiter's compartment.

Hurrying back into the house, he threw the net over the mad machine, which by this time

was spinning around in circles, spraying paint and paste everywhere! As the machine became tangled in the net, Sam leapt on top of it, and struck the control panel with the axe! **Bang!**

The Decorating Machine blew a fuse, and sparks showered over the room.

"This was why I brought the fire extinguisher," explained Sam to Penny, spraying the machine and the room with foam to stop any fires.

At last, the machine ground to a halt. Penny looked around at the mess - and chuckled. "You said

I'd be surprised when I saw my newly decorated living room, Sam," she laughed. "And you're right. I'm **very** surprised!"

Sam promised to clean up the mess, and to redecorate the room himself.

"It might take longer, but at least it will be done properly!" he laughed.

When Sam had finished, Penny invited him to stay for tea. It was Sam's **favourite** - jam and crumpets.

Plane Cooking!

It was a quiet afternoon at the station, so Sam was trying out a new invention. "This remote-controlled plane is great!"

Just then, Station Officer Steele shouted, "Jump to it, Sam. Fire at Pontypandy forest." Sam ran to Jupiter.

As they sped off, Sam realised that he had left his plane flying around. "Great fires of London. I hope it doesn't **crash!**"

Meanwhile, the plane nose-dived into Elvis Cridlington's kitchen. Elvis was listening to some music, so he didn't hear!

Soon the crew returned. "This has made me hungry," said Sam. "I hope Elvis has cooked something plain and simple!

"Er, something has happened to my pie," moaned Elvis. "Now that's what I call **plane** cooking!" sighed Sam.

Activity Time
Hat Mix-Up!

Oh dear! Everyone has the wrong hat on. Help them to find their own hat by drawing lines between each hat and it's rightful owner!

28

A Fireman Sam Story!

Elvis's Pancakes

Elvis makes a hit with his pancakes!

I'm going to make us some pancakes for our tea," Elvis Cridlington announced in the kitchen, to the loud groans of his fellow fire-fighters. "You won't be laughing when you taste my pancakes," he said, setting out his cooking equipment on the table.

"No, they will probably be so sticky, we won't be able to open our mouths to laugh!" teased Sam.

Elvis ignored his joke, and set to work. He poured the batter into a frying pan on a hot stove.

"**Great Fires of London!**" gasped Sam, as he sniffed the air. "Elvis has proven us wrong! Those pancakes smell **delicious!**"

"I told you so!" said Elvis, proudly. "And now I shall do my famous 'pan-cake flip!'" Elvis carefully lifted

the pan from the stove. The pancake was baked perfectly. "**Alley-oops!**" shouted Elvis, flipping the pancake into the air.

"Er, I thought the pancake was supposed to land back in the pan!" said Penny, when the pancake failed to appear.

She looked up, and there on the ceiling, was the pancake - **stuck fast!**

"Oh dear!" groaned Elvis. "That wasn't supposed to happen!"

"We can't eat that!" said Station Officer Steele. "We'll just have to go without pancakes for our tea!"

Just then, the 'phone rang. It was Norman Price. "My mum says she needs all the firefighters down the General Store at once!" he said, before ringing off.

"Action stations, men!" cried Steele. "This sounds like a real emergency!"

But when the firefighters reached the General Store in Jupiter, they were in for a surprise.

"There's no emergency!" said Dilys. "I just wanted you all to come and share our pancakes with us! I knew you wouldn't be able to eat Elvis's pancakes!"

"Huh! What a Cheek!" muttered Elvis. But even he had to admit that Dilys' pancakes **were** delicious!

It's Fun to Count on...
Pancake Day

There are lots of lovely things to count on Pancake Day.

lemons

eggs

bottles of milk

bags of flour

jars of jam

31

Join in the Pontypandy Pancake Race. All you need are dice and coloured counters. Throw the dice and move the number of pancakes shown. First to the finish wins the race!

Dot to Dot!

Norman has a new friend! Find out who it is. Join the dots and then colour in the picture!

Fireman Sam and Elvis are off to fetch the ...

Christmas Tree

One crisp and cool December morning, Fireman Sam was driving Jupiter along the quiet country roads outside Pontypandy. He and Elvis Cridlington had been given two very important tasks by Station Officer Steele. First, they had to pick up a new spare wheel for Venus, the fire tender. Secondly - and this was the job Sam was most looking forward to- they had to collect the Pontypandy Christmas Tree from the Nursery and transport it back to the village.

"Christmas is coming, and so is the Christmas Tree," smiled Elvis. "You know Sam, I think that Christmas is my favourite time of year."

"Mine too," Sam agreed, slowing the fire engine down as they came to a low bridge. "The only problem is," he went on, as they just squeezed through, "I can't decide what presents to give the twins this year. As their

easier to transport.

The tree was very large and heavy, so the Nursery workers helped the firemen lift it onto the engine's roof.

Even with the tree securely fastened to Jupiter's ladder, Sam had to drive back carefully to Pontypandy. But on the journey back, Sam suddenly braked and pulled into the side. He pointed along the road. "That's an even bigger problem than what to give the twins for Christmas," he sighed.

Sam was pointing to the low bridge which they'd

Uncle, I want to surprise Sarah and James with something that they haven't got, and won't be expecting."

After the two firemen had picked up the new wheel for Venus, they soon came to the Christmas Tree Nursery.

The special tree for Pontypandy was ready with its branches tied up to make it passed beneath earlier. They had to go back through it to get to Pontypandy, but with the large Christmas Tree on the roof, Jupiter just wouldn't fit under it this time.

"What are we going to do, Sam?" asked a troubled-looking Elvis. "The tree is too big and heavy for us to carry through to the other side."

Sam knew that Elvis was right but he also knew that they couldn't let everyone in the village down by failing to bring the Christmas Tree home. Sam frowned. If he'd been back in his Inventing Shed, he may have been able to build something to do the trick. Then Sam had an idea! **"Great fires of London!"** he cried. "We don't need my shed - everything we want is right **here!"**

"It **is**?" gasped Elvis. "Yes! Fetch Jupiter's spare wheel for me." Elvis did as he was asked, while Sam went to the side of the engine. He opened up the flap to a compartment which contained Jupiter's tool box, and pulled it out. Next, Sam rolled the new spare wheel that they had just collected for Venus to the back of the engine where Elvis was waiting, still very puzzled.

"We're going to fix the two spare wheels to the ladder, which has the

Christmas Tree fastened to it, "Sam told Elvis. "Then we lower the ladder to the ground, fasten it to the back of Jupiter and tow the Christmas Tree through the bridge..."

"...and **back** to **Pontypandy!**" added Elvis, catching on at last.

The two firemen worked quickly. Soon they had the wheels fitted to the ladder with the Christmas Tree on it. They were able to tow it under the low bridge, exactly as Sam had said.

"Pontypandy next stop!" grinned Elvis. "I just wish it was as easy to think of presents for Sarah and James."

"Oh, I already have," chuckled Sam. "What we've just done has given me an idea. I'm going to put **them** on wheels too!"

"But ...how on earth ...?" gasped Elvis, baffled by Sam's suggestion. This made Sam chuckle all the more.

"It's simple really," he said. "I'm going to buy them **roller skates!**"

Odd One Out!

One of these Christmas trees is the odd one out. It is not one of a pair. Find out which tree it is by matching the pairs!

To the Rescue

Norman is stuck up a tree! To rescue him you need a dice and counters. Throw the dice and move the number of squares shown. First to the tree wins the race!

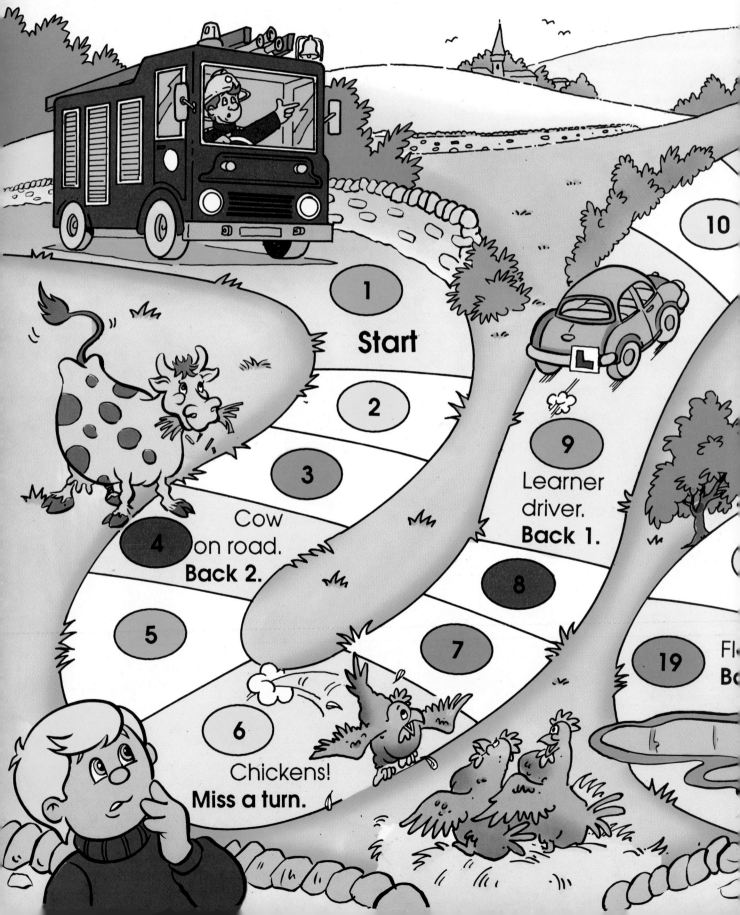

1
Start

2

3

4
Cow on road.
Back 2.

5

6
Chickens!
Miss a turn.

7

8

9
Learner driver.
Back 1.

10

19
Fl...
B...

Fireman for the Day!

" **J**upiter is looking very dirty," said Station Officer Steele to Sam and Elvis. "I want you to clean it."

Before Sam and Elvis could set to work, they met Norman who was playing at **'Fireman for the Day'**.

"As you're a fireman today," said Sam. "You can clean Jupiter. Here's a sponge and some clean water."

Norman was upset. "They just give me all the horrible jobs to do," he moaned. "I'm going home."

A Naughty Norman Story

Before Norman reached home, he saw smoke billowing out of Officer Steele's house. "Oh **no!** A **fire!**"

Norman went to a 'phone box and telephoned the Fire Station. "**Quickly**, sir," he said. "Your house is on **fire!**"

Station Officer Steele's toaster was alight. The firemen soon put the blaze out. "Good work," said Steele.

As a reward, Steele made Norman '**Station Officer for the Day**'. "Right men," said Norman. "Clean Jupiter."

the kittens?

Eight kittens have run away from the Pontypandy Cattery. Can you find them all for Fireman Sam?

PAINT NORMAN!

Hats Off!

It's Inspection Time at the Pontypandy Fire Station!

Station Officer Steele was planning an inspection of the Pontypandy Fire Station. Fireman Sam knew that everything would have to be spick and span, so he took off his tunic and helmet, placed them on the driver's seat in Jupiter, and set about giving the fire engine an extra special polish. It took him the whole morning, but, by the time Sam had finished, every inch of Jupiter gleamed!

"Better than new," Sam told himself, when he stood back to admire his work. "Now, I've just got time for a cup of tea

before the inspection."
Sam went inside, leaving
his tunic and helmet in
Jupiter's cab.

Naughty Norman
skipped up to the engine a
few moments later. He
expected to find Sam
inside, but saw only his
tunic and helmet. Norman
picked up the helmet and
tried it on for size. It was far
too big for Norman - it
slipped down over his ears,
and almost knocked his
glasses off his nose.

Norman pushed the
helmet up to look at the
engine. Its red body
dazzled, its silver bumpers
shone, and its golden bell
glinted. Then he had a
very naughty idea ...

A few moments later,
Norman peeped over a
nearby wall as Fireman
Sam hurried out to Jupiter.
"I took too long over my
tea," Sam said to himself.
"The inspection's about to
begin!"

Sam quickly pulled on
his tunic, and, as Elvis and
Trevor were lining up, he
reached for his helmet.
"Great Fires of London,"
gasped Sam - there was
something else on the seat
instead of his helmet.

bell should be?"

Sam didn't have an answer. Feeling very silly, he removed the bell from his head. Naughty Norman could contain himself no longer, and he started to giggle. Sam, hearing the sounds of laughter coming from behind the nearby wall, became very suspicious.

When Station Officer Steele left, Sam looked over the wall and saw Norman hiding on the other side. "I thought I recognised that laugh." said Sam. Norman chuckled. He was pleased that Sam had taken the joke so well.

In fact, Sam was planning to play a trick on Norman. "If you climb up on Jupiter and put the bell back where it belongs, I'll give you a fireman's hat all of your own."

"Great!" beamed Norman, who wasted no time in doing what Sam asked. While Norman was placing the bell back into the holder on the fire engine's roof, Sam nipped into the crew room for a

Officer Steele was coming out of the station. With no time to do anything else, Sam put the object on his head and lined up with the others.

Station Officer Steele soon noticed that Sam was not properly dressed. "Fireman Sam," he began sternly. "Why have you got Jupiter's bell on your head?" Officer Steele then glanced at Jupiter. "And why is your helmet on Jupiter, hanging where the

"Here it is," said Sam producing a funny hat that he'd made by folding up a sheet of newspaper.

Norman wasn't impressed. "What's that? Where's my helmet?"

"Who said anything about a helmet," Sam replied. "I promised you a fireman's hat, which is what you've got - a **hat** made by me, a **fireman**." Norman's face turned as red as Jupiter, for he realised he'd been had. "You see, Norman," chuckled Sam. "You're not the only one who can do hat tricks!"

sheet of newspaper. He was just coming out again when Norman dashed over carrying Sam's helmet.

"Thanks," smiled Sam, placing the helmet on his head. "Ahh, that's much better. I feel like a fireman again, instead of feeling silly."

Norman looked up eagerly at Sam. "Where's my fireman's hat?"

Fishing!

"Hello, you two," said Sam, when he met Sarah and James, one morning. "I'm going fishing. I'll catch a fish for tea!"

Sam headed for Pontypandy river and then unpacked his gear. Soon Sam had a bite, but it was just an old iron.

He put the iron behind him and started again. Then he had another bite - this time it was an old kettle. Sam groaned.

Later, Sarah and James dropped by to see how Sam was getting on. "You have nothing but junk," chuckled James.

This gave Sam an idea. He picked up all the junk he had caught and took them to the scrap yard.

Later, at Bella's, Sam laughed. "I didn't catch any fish, but I sold enough scrap metal to buy us a fish for supper!"

Early Snowfall!

Sam had invented a snow-making machine for the Pontypandy Drama Group's new play.

"I **love** snow," thought Norman when Sam left for work. "I'll just borrow Sam's machine for a while!"

Norman turned on the machine. Lots of thick, white, fake snow spurted out. "**Ha! Ha!** This is **fun!**"

Bella didn't think that it was fun! "**Waaah!**" she cried, slipping in the snow. "**Mama mia!**"

A Naughty Norman Story

Trevor wasn't very happy either. His bus skidded in the snow and finished up in the village flower bed!

Norman tried to switch off the machine - but nothing happened! "Oh dear! It's **broken**," he groaned.

Bella telephoned the fire brigade! "I'll fix it!" said Sam, turning off the machine by using a big hammer. **Bang!**

"And now you can fix this mess, Norman!" chuckled Sam, handing him a broom. "By sweeping it up!"

Spot the Difference

Can you spot the **10** differences between these 2 pictures?

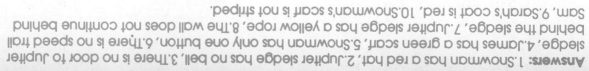

Answers: 1.Snowman has a red hat, 2.Jupiter sledge has no bell, 3.There is no door to Jupiter sledge, 4.James has a green scarf, 5.Snowman has only one button, 6.There is no speed trail behind the sledge, 7.Jupiter sledge has a yellow rope, 8.The wall does not continue behind Sam, 9.Sarah's coat is red, 10.Snowman's scarf is not striped.

The Brass Band

"Band concerts are boring," thought Naughty Norman. "I'll have to liven this one up!"

The firefighters were practising for the band recital concert in Pontypandy Park one afternoon.

"One, two, **three...**" shouted Station Officer Steele, waving his baton as the band began to play their instruments in the station yard.

Penny was playing the flute and Elvis the tuba, while Trevor blew the trumpet and Sam banged the big, bass drum.

"**Boom-biddy-boom, biddy-boom!**"

Station Officer Steele smiled as he brought the baton down to end the practice session. "First class!" he said. "The villagers of Pontypandy are in for a concert that they won't forget!"

"It certainly should!" giggled Norman, who was hiding behind the bandstand.

At two o'clock, everyone arrived, and the band concert began. Dilys, Bella, Sarah, and James clapped along to the music.

No one noticed Norman climb onto the bandstand behind Elvis. He

Naughty Norman Price was peering around the wall, looking into the yard. He gave a mischievous chuckle. "Hah! Hah! Band concerts are **boring**. I'll have to think of something to liven this one up!"

That afternoon, the firefighters arrived in the park in Jupiter. Chairs had been put out to face the bandstand for people to sit on.

"I'm looking forward to this," said Sam, as the firefighters tuned their instruments. "It should be a lot of fun!"

held a big, hairy, trick spider in his hand, which he dropped inside Elvis's tuba.

Elvis blew the tuba - **BARRRP!** - and the spider flew out again and landed on Penny's flute.

"**Eeek!**" she screamed, throwing her flute across the bandstand. It struck Trevor on the nose.

"**Ouch**" he cried, falling back and knocking over Sam's drum. The drum rolled off the bandstand and down the grassy hill.

"**Come back!**" cried Sam, chasing after it. The drum rolled up the other side of the hill, and then rolled back again towards Sam.

"Oh **no! Run!**" cried Sam, running off in the opposite direction chased by the drum. Everyone scattered as the drum smashed into the chairs, knocking them over.

Norman laughed and laughed. It was the funniest thing he had ever seen.

He was so busy thinking what a clever trick he had played that he didn't notice the drum heading his way.

"**Eeek!**" he squealed, when the heavy drum knocked him flying into the air. He landed headfirst in the tuba Elvis was holding!

"I can't play my tuba with your head in it, Norman!" Elvis said angrily. "Pull it out again!"

"I **can't,**" came the muffled reply. "It's **stuck!**"

"**Great Fires of London!**" chuckled Sam, when he saw the tuba stuck on Norman's head. "What will the lad get up to **next?**"

Station Officer Steele took command. "**Action Stations!** The removal of one tuba from Master Price's head to commence! Take hold and - **pull!**"

58

Sam and Trevor took hold of the tuba, and Penny and Elvis took hold of Norman. They pulled very hard.

With a loud plop Norman was pulled free. He popped out so fast, everyone fell back on the ground in a heap.

"Humph! Now it's time for you to face the music, young Price," said a very cross Station Officer. "For trying to ruin our band concert, you can serve tea to everyone - and then you can pick up all the litter in the park!"

"This is **awful!**" groaned Norman later, after he had walked around the park filling a sack with rubbish. "My poor aching back! Next time, I'll just sit and watch the band concert like everyone else. No more tricks for me!"

Do **you** think that naughty Norman meant it? **No?** Nor did Fireman Sam!

Activity Time!

Lost!

James and Sarah are lost in the woods. Help Fireman Sam to find them by finding the right path for him to follow.

There are **5 squirrels** hiding i the woods. Can you **find** ther